Bad Dates

by Theresa Rebeck

SAMUEL FRENCH

FOUNDED 1830

New York Hollywood London Toronto

SAMUELFRENCH.COM

ISBN   978-0-573-63047-7   Printed   in   U.S.A.   #4900

IMPORTANT BILLING AND CREDIT REQUIREMENTS

All producers of BAD DATES *must* give credit to the Author of the Play in all programs distributed in connection with performances of the Play and in all instances in which the title of the Play appears for purposes of advertising, publicizing or otherwise exploiting the Play and/or a production. The name of the Author *must* appear on a separate line on which no other name appears, immediately following the title, and *must* appear in size of type not less than fifty percent the size of the title type.

BAD DATES

by

Theresa Rebeck

was originally produced Off Broadway
in the Spring of 2003 by
Playwrights Horizons
Tim Sanford, *Artistic Director.*

Cast

Haley   Julie White

Directed by John Benjamin Hickey

Scenic design by Derek McLane
Costume design by Mattie Ullrich
Lighting design by Frances Aronson
Sound design by Bruce Ellman

Production State Manager Megan Schneid
Production Manager Joshua Helman

CHARACTERS

HALEY: Late 30's/early 40s, a restaurant manager.

SET

Haley's bedroom in an apartment in New York City. It is a friendly, warm space, not frilly. At the top of the play there are clothes thrown everywhere, and a lot of shoes, a very, very lot of shoes. Upstage right is the door to Haley's bathroom. Stage left is the door to the hall leading to another bedroom: the unseen domain of Vera, Haley's daughter.

SCENE 1

(A woman, HALEY, stands alone, in her bedroom. It is a friendly, warm space, not frilly. There are clothes thrown everywhere, and a lot of shoes, a very very lot of shoes, although the shoes are not in piles. She handles them with some care.)

HALEY.
Do you like these shoes? They're cute, right?

(Dissatisfied, she throws them down and goes to pick through several pairs that are on the bed. She starts to put them on.)

I can't wear shoes anymore. You know, it's not that you can't wear them, but you start to go, oh god these things hurt, it's like having your foot stuck in a bear trap.

(She goes down the hallway, calls.)

Vera! Hey, come look at these. Come on, it's a big night for me. *(A doorway opens, the sound of teen music. HALEY yells over it)* Do you think these are cute? These are cute, right? Oh. Well. No. You're right, you're right. They hurt, anyway.

(The music stops as Vera's door is shut. Haley hobbles back into her bedroom.)

7

Listen, I haven't looked at these things in years. It's not like I have a fetish or anything. I mean, I know that it looks like I have a fetish. Well, I do have a fetish, but it's not like some crazy Imelda Marcos fetish, although I admit it might look like that.

(She looks at a pair of shoes in a box, then shows them to the audience.)

These aren't as cute as I thought. Joan and David. Remember when you thought they were cute, and now they're not, they're just not hip enough? It's 'cause the name isn't good enough, that's what I think. Jimmy Chou, much cuter name and sure enough the shoes are cute in a timelessly cute way. *(Off the dagger-like heel.)* Well, maybe not cute. They look like you could stab someone with this heel, don't they, what is that about? Anyway, I used to live six blocks from this shoe store in Austin, George's shoe store, I kid you not that was the name, not very glamorous, the name or the store, which was kind of a little dump but this guy George had some sort of a deal with all these major shoe designers and he got their leftovers, which he sold at rock bottom prices out of this icky little hole in the wall. This place was a miracle. Everything he sold was something like twenty or thirty bucks, I am dead serious, you could go down there at least once a week and pick up a three hundred dollar pair of Chanel pumps for a mere thirty dollars. Well, you couldn't do that every week, that only happened to me once, but it was an unforgettable day, as you may imagine. Here they are....

(She holds them up, jubilant.)

Okay. A little conservative but still unspeakably chic. Thirty bucks. But you had to have the right size foot. Six to seven and a half, that was mostly what he sold, that's mostly what the leftovers were, your foot's bigger than that you are mostly out of luck. I took one of my friends there, she's a size nine, she had to go outside and have a good cry. Anyway, the other cool thing about this astonishing little store, there was a lady's spike heel shoe, huge, it was like size eleven or something, and someone had glued little macaronis all over this shoe, and then spray painted it brown, and it was in the window. It looked like something a kid would have done, and then to be nice, his dad put it in his store window. So I was very touched by this shoe, even though the color it was spray painted was kind of an icky brown. If you're going to go to all the trouble with the macaroni, wouldn't you think to paint it lime green, or sparkles or something? Anyway—oh ow. Oh no. Oh no....

(She has on the Chanel pumps, which are too tight.)

Dammit, they shrank. Shoes don't shrink. My feet grew. Oh shoot. They're not that cute anyway. Yes, oh yes they are. Oh I'm going to just weep. Shoot. Maybe I'll just frame them, or something. Anyway this shoe store, you just couldn't resist—

(She opens a box and, surprised, sees a huge wad of cash.)

Oh wow, well, this does not belong with the shoes now does it?

(She packs it back up and puts the shoebox under the bed.)

Anyway, I ended up with some pretty strange shoes, I'll admit, zebra stripe half boots, gold lame spikes, you know, stuff you just think is too wild to pass up, maybe the occasion or the outfit will someday present itself. And George was nice, and I'm moved as I said by the shoe with the macaronis. So I end up with this huge collection of shoes for very little money. And I was pregnant. The two things really didn't have much to do with each other, although I'm sure I was wearing something in this mess the night Vera was conceived. Whatever. So the next thing I know I have six hundred pairs of shoes, a husband—Roger—and a kid. And then things start disappearing around the house, including the Toyota, which Roger has traded for three pounds of marijuana. I hope you don't think ill of me for admitting all this. Because I am not that person anymore, having a child makes some of us grow up. Not all of us, Roger being the relevant case in point. I'm going to weep I am just going to weep, do none of these fit? What kind of cruel universe would do that to me? So the next thing I know I'm a divorced waitress with a five-year-old kid—see these are cute, and they fittttt.

(She looks at herself in the shoes in the mirror.)

Yeah they're cute, of course they're cute, they belong to my daughter. I look like a thirteen year old in them.

(She starts to take them off.)

(Yelling to door.) Hey Vera, I found your blue buckle shoes! *(She takes them to Vera's room, quickly, then returns.)* Anyway, we move to New York, Vera and I. Fresh start. We're in the big city, getting by, you know, I got a nice little job as a waitress. I found this amazing apartment—rent controlled! And things are looking up, definitely, when it turns out this restaurant I'm working at is some kind of front, some Romanian mob put all their money in it as a tax shelter or money laundering, I can't even, believe me, you didn't want to know, at that point I was raising a five year old and the less I knew about—

(She starts in on another pair, very high heels.)

I'm mostly hoping the feds or the police or whoever don't find out whatever illegal activity is going on, because I don't want to lose my job. Then sure enough—ow, god, ow—

(She walks around.)

Okay, these hurt but they fit.

(She continues to walk, looks at herself in the mirror.)

I'm sorry this story is taking so long. Because it's just of course the police do figure out something—I think it was money laundering—

(She starts to change her clothes, into a snaky little dress.)

—Which I of course suspected, and then have to lie about when all these detectives descend and ask how much you know. I felt like such a terrible person. They had this whole complicated sting worked out, one of those things that they spent years setting up, so you know they've been working for years figuring out something you knew all along. But you can't really feel sorry for them because why the hell did it take them so long? Besides which they're being kind of pushy and snotty around the restaurant, making us all wait in the back, where there's no place to sit, and not telling anyone what's going on, my little girl is with her baby sitter and I'm not even allowed to call, and all of us, we're all like great, there goes my job, and finally I say to one of them, the cops, What's going on, anyway? And he's like, some big macho, when we need to talk to you, we will let you know. And there is so much creepy attitude, I mean, this is our lives he's messing with and he's just some big old nasty cop. So I say to him, look, is this about the money laundering thing? And he sort of looks at me, all surprised, and says Oh you know all about that, huh. And I said, well, isn't it common knowledge? At which point one of the cooks offers me a cigarette, just to get me to shut up. I mean, I admit I was being a bit stupid, they had already taken Veljko off in handcuffs. We all of course felt that it was about time somebody did—Veljko was just a big fat criminal, there was no question, big and fat and mean, he looked like Al Capone or a cardinal or something, and it was a huge relief someone finally arrested him, but my point is, this was clearly a serious matter, I had no business mouthing off to anybody about anything.

(She looks at herself in the mirror.)

Okay, that looks good. Right? This is very good. I look like a hooker.
Well, maybe I can wear this with a scarf. You know, look like a
hooker wearing a scarf or something.

(She starts to look for a scarf.)

So then, all the guys who are running the restaurant are completely
arrested but then the family, which as it turns out not all of them, apparently, are mobbed up, you know how those things work, there's
always like a couple who are not complete criminals but they can call
up the complete criminals when they need a favor. So that side of the
family decides to keep the place open, but they have no idea how anything works and a new one shows up every night, so I'm the one ends
up walking them all through it cause I seem to be the only one who
knows anything about how the place works. Everybody else there is
so concentrated on their own little piece of turf no one knows anything about the whole place, except me. So, you know, the non criminal Romanians finally go to hell with it, and put me in charge, because apparently I'm sort of weird restaurant idiot savant. Who knew?
Born to run a restaurant. Which is exciting. When you find something,
some strange combination of, who you are and what you can do, to
find your gift like that? How many people get that to fall on their head
like that? 'Cause I started out being like just a waitress trying to sup-
port herself and her kid, I mean I was just another person who married
a moron and then had a load of shit to deal with. *(Off outfit, in mirror.)* Yeah okay, this is a clear disaster but I do like the top.

(She starts to take off the skirt.)

So things are swinging. I'm allowed to do things that nobody else
ever thought of, add stuff to the menu, change the layout of the place
and get rid of the lousy flatware, you know, plus I went out and stole
somebody's chef, not the nicest thing I've ever done, but they were
abusing him over there, I mention no names, but chefs are artists. You

treat them nicely. And the next thing I know—'cause this stuff happens so fast you can't even, you would not believe and I mean that— get reviewed in *The New York Times*, it's a rave, and Leonardo DiCaprio throws his birthday party at my restaurant and we make Page Six! And business goes through the roof. Which could not be more fun.

So I'm feeling fantastic, because there is nothing better in life than being allowed to do a job that you're good at, so guys are asking me out all the time. I mean I am *en fuego*, and I don't actually have time to date, between the restaurant and Vera, so I'm turning them all down, which makes 'em want me even more! But I'm thinking, there's got to be a way to work this out, I miss sex, it would be fun to have someone to talk to, besides Vera, who is a great kid but let's face it she's seven by that point and I'm hitting my sexual prime. So I'm contemplating this, I'm ready, there's this guy hanging around who seems like a good possibility, you know, he's nice, and funny, and great looking in this skinny way. You know how great looking skinny guys are sometimes? So he's showing up at the restaurant two or three nights a week, just to have a drink and flirt. And this is very high end flirting, you know, when he says something snappy, and you hand it right back to him only better and then float away to show somebody to their table, and then curve back around the bar for another dazzling four second encounter, it was sooo sexy, and he finally asks me out, and I am yes yes yes. I mean, I like this guy, I really—He—whatever. The thing is, right then—right then, this friend of mine, Eileen, sees this Joan Crawford marathon on some movie channel. And she comes over the restaurant laughing her fool head off, and says have you seen Mildred Pierce? 'Cause Haley, it is you. She thinks this is this big hilarious blinding insight, cannot stop laughing, so I rent the video. You know, I go out, I rent the video, and I watch it.

(HALEY looks at the audience. Beat.)

Okay. Have you seen Mildred Pierce? Joan Crawford, gorgeous, competent, devoted to her kids, husband turns out to be kind of a loser, so she goes out and gets a job—as a waitress. She's got no training, does it because she has to, and turns out to be—well, you know, kind of a restaurant idiot savant, gets her own place, it's a huge hit, she doesn't have time to date but men are falling all over her so she finally starts to date them and terrible terrible things happen, and everything goes to shit. I mean, I am not making this up. That is what happens in this movie I truly, I mean, oh lord. And oh, get this. The kid's name? She has an evil daughter? Veda. My kid's name is Vera.

And they are nothing alike, Vera is really a good kid, she's more like the tragic daughter who dies, but still. On top of it, this guy who's been sniffing around, asking me out, is just a dead ringer for Monty, the evil socialite who Mildred marries and who steals from her and then destroys her and seduces her daughter. I mean— Okay, he didn't look exactly like him, but they were both skinny. And I just went, no, I got my restaurant, I got my kid, for the first time in my whole life I got enough money so I'm not worried about it every waking moment of every single day. I am not tempting fate.

(She is now dressing herself in much more conservative clothing, a long skirt, and a sweater.)

I mean—I'm not saying watching that movie five years ago made me realize I couldn't have a man in my life. It just made me think. So I said NO to Monty and I did without. And you know, it's all right, everybody has to do without something in their lives. A lot of people have to do without the work that they love, I know people, can't get a job, doing the thing that they love, and it's a wound that they carry. You know, really, a great sadness. I think that would be a bigger loss, frankly. 'Cause I have family, my kid is fantastic, and I have friends. My friend Eileen, she doesn't have a boyfriend or a kid, plus for the longest time she was always in and out of work, she's a, one of those, you know—she paints, or photography, or film something—she really is a genius, but she never seems to land somewhere where they'll just let her do what she does, whatever that is at the time. It's hard. And she drinks, you know. Well, why not....

(She goes down the hall to Vera's room.)

Vera! Come look at this! *(Over Vera's music.)* Don't just make a face. I'm real nervous. Tell me what you think, is it the skirt? Don't tell me what you think. You're thirteen, what do you know.

(The music stops. HALEY comes back into her bedroom.)

She's right, this skirt is way too something, who knows what. *(She adds a belt.)* Anyway Eileen. Once things worked out for me at the restaurant I gave her a job of course, what else can you do with somebody like that, it's not what she wants to do but at least she's working for someone who loves her, and she's a pretty good bartender, no surprise there. So last week, this is what happened: Eileen gets us invited to this benefit for Tibetan Buddhist books. I kid you not. She has a friend who said we could come to this thing for free, which seems to me like no way to run a benefit, but apparently it's more common than you would think. So this "benefit" is out on the Island, so we take the train out there. And sure enough everyone is walking around this gorgeous estate, talking about Tibetan Buddhist books. Acres and acres of lawn and huge trees and this gorgeous sprawling mansion and people dressed in traditional Buddhist robes serving brie with sundried tomatoes, and glasses of chardonnay to everybody. And then the celebrities start to arrive. Not a lot—Janet Leigh, of all people, shows up, and then a couple of television stars who I didn't know who they were. And then people start to say, Richard Gere is coming, Richard Gere is coming, but he never came.

(She starts to go through her makeup, looking for lip gloss, puts it on as she continues with the story.)

So anyway, they finally seat us at tables which are scattered about this gorgeous lawn. Now the thing is, Eileen, as I said, got us into this thing for free because a friend of hers is on the committee, and they need people to fill out tables. So they basically split us up. And I get seated at this table, the kindest thing, the only thing to say about this table, is that it is the table of the weirdos.

Real nuts, every one of them, so I decide I need to act very normal, and I say, Hi, I'm Haley Walker, I mention the restaurant, blah, blah, blah, and this old lady starts talking about bugs, and how she's trying to communicate with bugs. Some famous Buddhist told her to do that, and suddenly the entire table is having a seemingly endless conversation about how when a mosquito lands on your arm you should become one with it, rather than flicking it off before it gives you encephalitis.

(She rolls her eyes.)

Then it starts to rain, just a little, and the lady who owns the house, who doesn't want to let us in her house for some reason, gets up and starts talking about how the rain is a gift of the Buddha. So we're all sitting there, getting rained on, thinking about how it's a gift of the Buddha, and then it starts to rain really hard, and the lady who's house it is suggests we all put our napkins on our heads. So all of us are sitting there with napkins on our heads, getting rained on, including Janet Leigh.

(She stops, looks at herself. She looks very nice. She bites her lip, goes back to the piles of shoes and starts to look again, for a pair that goes with her lovely but staid outfit.)

So it's raining and raining and we're all getting rained on, but the conversation about bugs just keeps going. And there's this guy sitting next to the old lady who started the whole thing, who cannot get enough of this. He is positively fascinated by her stories about talking to bugs.

And then he turns to me and says, "Have you ever tried it?" No shit. And the entire table, all the weirdos turn and are all looking at me with deep and real, serious-minded expectation. There is a hush, an absolute, definite hush. So I say, "No, I am not friendly with the insect world but there are several amphibians with whom I play golf regularly." And then they all continue to stare at me, but now there's a kind of shocked disappointment that gathers in the silence. And I confess, you know, I think I may have let a little bit of an edge creep into my voice, when I said it, so I guess I did communicate that talking to nut jobs about bugs in the middle of a thunderstorm was not especially my idea of a good time.

(She sighs, remembering her own bad behavior.)

So then the bug guy, you know, the one who attempted to drag me into this in the first place—he says to me, "So ... what's a frog's handicap, these days?" And I mutter, "The ones I play with are pretty much scratch golfers," and the old lady gets huffy about not understanding golf and goes back to the damn bugs and the hope that all sentient beings might someday come to enlightenment. And then I think oh dear god, they're not talking about the bugs now, they're talking about me. It was completely mortifying. So I'm sitting there, feeling bad, and wet, and like a bug, and then I realize, in this sort of strange, hallucinatory moment, that the bug guy is looking kind of good, and the things he's saying about bugs are really kind of fascinating— and it is then that I realize that maybe it has been too long since I've been on a date. When the bug guy starts looking good, it's time to get out of the house.

(Beat.)

Tonight, I'm going on a date.

(Blackout.)

SCENE 2

*(HALEY is in her robe, with a towel on her head. She is eating a pret-
zel and on the phone, on her bed.)*

No I am not wearing that. B.J.—I look like a slut in that dress. Yes,
you were the one who told me at Sue Jane's wedding, it was the first
time I wore it and you said I was the only one who wasn't dressed like
a chicken, AND I looked like a slut. *(Laughing.)* What, the one with
the little sleeves? I hate those sleeves. B.J., that has polka dots.
You're no help at all. I have to go, I have to figure out how to look
sexy without looking like a slut. I can too. Can too. Can too. Tell
Frank I said hi. I don't know why he likes you. Bye bye, brother.

*(She hangs up the phone and starts to lay outfits out on the bed, this
time trying tops and skirts and shoes together, like Barbie out
fits.)*

(To audience.) All right, that first date was not what you would call a
success. It was a bad date. I'm obviously out of practice, and having
decided to date again as a matter of necessity, I went out with the first
guy who asked and it was just a matter of getting my feet wet. What's
that terrible thing they used to say, about kissing, you have to kiss a
lot of frogs before you find a prince. What a thing to teach girls.
Not that I kissed this guy. Okay, I did kiss him, and he was an asshole, but by that point I was just trying to get out of the entire predica-
ment and just go home and get to bed, so one kiss seemed a small
price to pay. Regardless of the fact that there was tongue involved.

(She rolls her eyes and tosses all the clothes together, shoves them

into a laundry basket, and kicks it.)

Oh for heaven's sake, it's not like I don't do this every day anyway. You know, dress?

But that is where things went off, right at the beginning, after all that messing around I did with my clothes, the first thing out of that guy's mouth, the very first thing he says to me was, "What are you wearing?" Can you believe that? My mother used to do that to me. And I say to him, why? What's wrong with it? And he says, "It just makes you look kind of old." That was the beginning. Now, I know I've been out of the game for a while, and I'm not in my twenties anymore but you have got to be kidding me, men are out there, running around, thinking that shit's okay. I'm not even—this guy is over forty, of course men at forty are considered the hottest thing going. And I'm like—what difference does it make how old I am. The point is, I am not as old as him.

(She sighs, and starts to dress, still eating pretzels. The outfit she chooses this time is considerably sexier.)

So after that spectacular opening we go to—I picked the restaurant, trust me, I know, I mean, right? You go out on a date with me, the thing to do is let me pick the restaurant and this place is nice, a high end bistro so it's not outrageous, but the food is delicious—there's only two things on the menu that are not worth trying, the calf's liver, and okay, they actually do a cow's head, which, I'm sorry, but this is America, nobody is going to order that. Anyway, so there we are, bad start but the restaurant could not be lovelier, candlelight, flowers— Beautiful.

The service is excellent, the wine, a ninety-five Bordeaux, I pick it because I know this stuff and it's just a lovely bottle with so many colors, berries and chocolate and just the right hint of smokiness around the edges, you know, it's almost an Amarone but it's French, it's one of those bottles that have no right to exist and yet there they are. So everything that I have contributed to this evening, I think, is rather good. This is a date I think many people would like to go on. And this guy is sitting there, looking at the menu and says, there's probably butter in all this stuff, isn't there?

(Beat. She looks at the audience, pissed.)

It's a goddamn French restaurant! Of course there's butter! And then we go down the list, item by item we study the menu and he talks about every single one of these positively brilliant offerings to the God of Food, and he wonders what might be in it, you know, "Do you think that has cream in it?" And he turns up his nose at it all and talks about how bad cream and butter are, and then I hear about his cholesterol. *(Beat.)* Let me tell you something. The first topic on a first date should not be cholesterol. Besides which I'm sitting there thinking, then order the salmon! How is this a real subject? If you're worried about your cholesterol, then order the fish! It's grilled! It says right on the menu, all our fish are grilled! BUT NO. We have to have an endless—and all of it, you know, is complicated by some sort of neurosis he has about numbers. Like, the normal number for a man his age would be this, but his doctor feels that his muscle mass is more appropriate to a younger man—of course he found a doctor out there who told him he wasn't as old as he actually is—so they calculated the cholesterol according to some other schedule and then sub-selected half of the difference, blah blah blah, so that means he has to watch his cholesterol but not really. So then, I kid you not, he orders the coquille Saint Jacques—scallops, wrapped in bacon, swimming in cream sauce, topped with toasted cheese.

And then through the entire first course, we continue to talk about cholesterol, only then we move on to his colon, apparently his battle with cholesterol has had an extremely negative impact on his COLON.

So I got to hear about that, and I will spare you the details, although he did not. *(Beat.)* So I'm like, okay, this is just a date that's not going to work out. That's obvious and it's not the end of the world, frankly, I didn't actually think the first guy I went out with would be "the one for me" or anything like that, I was just trying to go on a date. So I'm okay with the fact that this is largely pretty damn stupid. And then, there's actually a point in the evening where having completely given up on this guy I sort of perversely got interested in his story. He starts talking about his ex-girlfriend. And the more he talks about her, the clearer it becomes that he's still, really, kind of in love with her. And the more I listen to him, the more I realize that this is more or less a first date for him, too, he's recently broken up with this woman he really loved, and now he's trying to get back on the horse. And this thought honestly makes me feel a little warmly toward him, I sense that we are fellow-travelers. And so I say to him, as a fellow traveler, well, why did you break up? And he tells me this story about how— that your relationship with a person is like a movie. That when you're in a relationship, you see the movie, in your head, and that you need to see how the rest of the movie is going to go. And he realized that he couldn't see where the movie was going. He didn't know the end of the movie, with this woman. So he had to break up with her. And he looked so sad. Meanwhile, I'm listening to this, and trying to understand, so I say, What do you mean, a movie? And he goes through the whole thing again, about looking for the end of the movie, and your life with someone, and the relationship, and the end of the movie, so I say, you mean like death? Looking for the end of the movie, you're thinking about dying? And he says, No no no, it's not about death. It's about the End of the Movie. And we go around in circles like that for a while, and finally I say to him, I don't know, is it possible that you broke up with the woman you loved because of some insane metaphor?

And then he got mad at me. I don't blame him. I definitely was getting too personal. And I honestly had a moment when I thought, if you're siding with the guy's ex-girlfriend? It's not a good date. So then things were uncomfortable, and they kind of went from bad to worse, and by the end of the evening we were really annoyed with each other, and I let him stick his tongue in my mouth, anyway.

(She shakes her head, and goes looking for shoes again, piling a whole lot of them on the bed. She picks out two pair and steps into the hall, knocks on Vera's door. Vera's music comes up.)

Vera! I need you to tell me what shoes to wear. These are the only choices. Good. Thanks. What? Well, can't you wear the blue skirt with, that top you have on right now is so cute, I think—you know, people don't really care about your clothes, Vera. Who you are on the inside is much more important than what … oh, never mind.

(She goes back into the room for a moment, and looks under her bed. She takes out a large shoe box, opens it, takes out a huge wad of cash, peels off several bills, then closes the box and pushes it back under the bed. She tucks several bills into her own purse, then goes to Vera's room.)

(Continuing; off.) This is all I can spare this week, so you're going to have to shop at Contrampo for once, or T.J. Maxx, it was good enough for me so—

(She closes the door to Vera's room and comes back into her bedroom.)

Where was I? Oh. Right. Out in front of my building with Mr. Wonderful. There we are. Horrible, horrible evening, from start to finish, and yet he clearly expects to come up. I should have paid for myself, I offered, but I should have insisted because then you have a little more latitude to evade, you know, but I didn't, so I didn't have latitude, and there you have it. I am stuck with his tongue down my throat. It just, I have to say it shook me up, frankly, how quickly things progressed with this guy, on a date which was not by any means successful. I am not a prude, I think that's obvious but let's face it we clearly did not LIKE each other, but he was willing to sleep with me anyway! He was absolutely planning on it! What is that? Don't you think that's interesting, I think this is a true and extremely interesting point about the differences between the sexes: Men will happily have sex with someone they don't like. Women won't. Obviously that's not a hundred percent true, but kind of it is, and why? Why are men sleeping with people they don't like? Is sex that much more fun for men than women, that they'd do it with just anyone? That would be one conclusion. The other would be that maybe men don't have enough to think about. Oh well, I'm not one to talk, I let someone I didn't like at all stick his tongue in my mouth.

(She sighs and looks at herself in the mirror. She is dressed in a very snakey little number, and looks really really hot.)

Now that's not bad for a woman who's as old as I am, I would say. If my mother saw me tonight, and said, "Are you going to wear that?" She would not mean you look old. She would mean go right back in there and take that off young lady. But I am not dressing to please my mother. I have another date.

(Blackout.)

SCENE 3

(HALEY stands, in the same clothes, facing the audience. The room is as she left it—a mess.)

All right. I would just like to take this opportunity to admit that perhaps I have been, to some degree, indulging in male-bashing. And apologize to any men present, or even not present, for whatever amount of ill-humor, which may have offended you. Because tonight was an unmitigated disaster.

(She sits as she tries to explain.)

This is what happened: I get to the restaurant. Now, the fact is, this time, it's a blind date. Which I don't generally, I am well aware that there is an entire subculture of people getting together with total strangers for fun and companionship, but that is not something I am as yet interested in. At the same time, after my last fiasco, I didn't actually think it was such a great idea to just go on a date with someone who asked me. I wanted some background, research, other people invested in the outcome. So, okay, I was talking to my mom on the phone, and I did in fact do a stupid thing and mentioned to her that I was starting to date, and kind of just, looking for guys, you know, to date. I actually said that to my mother. Who seemed sort of interested, in a casual, motherly way, and then called me back fourteen minutes after we hung up the phone, having already entirely arranged my next date. Okay. Now, I did, for a moment, protest, because you know, who wants to go out on a date that their mother set up?

But then I'm thinking, well, she made him sound kind of good, actually. He's from San Antonio, so he's Texan in a good way, you know, Texas but not too macho, and he's been living in New York four years. He's a professor. He teaches at Columbia. He's a professor at the law school at Columbia. So I'm thinking—okay, I admit it: In spite of the fact that my mother set this date up, I am thinking George Stephanopolous with a cute southern accent. And I make no apologies for that. I have always believed that one should live with hope. So I call him up. And his accent is damn cute. He suggests that we go to my restaurant. I'm thinking well, that's like having dinner at home, far as I'm concerned, plus things are a little tense down there since I fired one of the busboys, Bibi, which was oh so necessary but always upset people, so I was looking forward to a night off. But then he goes on, how he's heard the place is so great and he's always wanted to go there and what a privilege it would be to dine with the artist who designed the entire experience.

(She takes a moment, pointing up the unmitigated pleasure of this.)

Okay. He called me an artist. So I'm going, yes! We can have dinner at the restaurant. I certainly know the wine cellar there, and this is a man who will appreciate the bottle of wine I am going to pick out for him. This man teaches in the Law School at Columbia. He may or may not look like George Stephanopolos. And we're going to have a good conversation about civil rights, the supreme court, I don't actually know what kind of law he teaches and I don't care 'cause the point is, I'm not going to be talking about colonoscopys all night.

And I'm not going to make the mistake of looking ten years older than I actually am on this date. So I get myself dressed—I am dressed, am I not? And I go to the restaurant.

(She starts to act this out.)

And Eileen, she's as I said, the bartender but nights I'm not in, she does the front desk. So she says to me, your friend is waiting at the bar. And she has a kind of great look in her eye, Eileen is a connoisseur, so I go oh boy, this guy is way cute. So I'm feeling good now, and I go to the bar to meet my date, and ... he's gay. He's cute, but he's also—gay. I mean, I am not—but he's gay! I am on a date with a gay man! And I mean, look, he's the kind of person, you can tell when you meet him. You shake his hand, he's gay. I'm thinking, why did my mother send me on a date with a gay man? Oh what a stupid question that is. And I am really mad at my mother for a moment, and then I'm thinking well why is he having his mother set

him up on dates with straight women? Has he not told his mother
yet? Does he possibly think she doesn't know? Maybe she doesn't
know, which brings us back to why hasn't he told her? He's got ten-
ure at Columbia and he can't tell his mom he dates boys? And then
I'm also thinking, even if you can't tell your mom because of whatever, that doesn't necessarily mean you let her set you up on dates
with girls!

(She sits, fuming.)

And then I'm thinking— *(Gestures to her snakey outfit.)* Wasted.
Snakiest outfit I've worn in eight years, wasted. And I looked good,
man, I thought I really looked good.

(She sighs, stares at the ceiling for a moment, starts to undress.)

So, there was a bad moment, right at the beginning, that I don't think
either one of us ever really recovered from. 'Cause I am sure that my
disappointment was to some degree palpable. Well, I was on a date
with a gay man!

Of course I was disappointed! And then he clearly thought, oh look at
this stupid pathetic straight woman, desperate to get laid by someone
who could not be less interested, but how was I to know that? I don't
know what he thought. Because we both got real polite real fast. I had
Eileen show us to our table and I order a great merlot. I mean, I'm
trying now, to be lovely, while I regroup, and he's attentive and ap-
preciative, but a little tense, you know. So then I'm thinking for half a
second, well, maybe he's disappointed because he saw that I was disappointed, so maybe he doesn't know he's gay. Or maybe he's not
gay and I'm doing one of those horrible snap judgment things, people
say you can always tell, but I don't think that's necessarily true. My
brother B.J.'s gay, and nobody had a clue, when he told me I thought
he was pulling my leg.

(She puts her hand over her face, remembering.)

Oh, it was horrible, he told me and I laughed, and he kept saying "no really" and I swear I just kept laughing 'cause that's kind of his sense of humor to do something like that, but this time he wasn't—anyway, it was just horrible. He got me back, though, 'cause he was too big a chicken to tell mom, so I had to tell her for him, which was—. Anyway. So I'm thinking now, maybe you can't tell, maybe this guy just seems gay, but really he's just a nice sensitive person with excellent taste, who teaches at Columbia and is unmarried at forty-three, and says, "what a privilege it would be to dine with the artist who designed the entire experience."

(She rolls her eyes; she knows this sounds dumb. She picks up the phone and starts to dial.)

So me thinking maybe I've leapt to a wrong conclusion lasts for maybe twenty seconds, which is about when I notice that he's flirting with the waiter. And then I just have to give myself over to it, just say okay, tonight I am on a date with a gay man.

(Into phone.) Hey B.J. it's me. Get this. You know that date mom set me up on? He was a big old homo. I know! *(Starting to laugh along with him.)* No yes he was cute, he was just no fun. Of course as long as she was looking, mom would find the least fun homosexual in the world. No I'm not giving you his number he was too mean. You have to ask Mom for it. Byyye.

(She hangs up, laughing.)

So anyway, the fact is Mr. Columbia Law Professor, whether or not he is gay, which he is, is finally less pertinent than the fact that he's snotty and kind of mean. He asks me how old I am, which I decline to answer, because I'm sorry, he's on a pretend date with a girl. It's rude even on a real date! So I just come out and say I'm not telling you that and he says, why, is it a problem for you? Can you imagine? I ask him what he teaches, and he says "law." I'm not kidding. "Law." So I say, yeah, my mom told me that part, what kind of law? And he says, "It's pretty technical." And then he just keeps reading the menu. So then I just say, well, what, you think I'm too damn stupid to understand? And he gives me this look, offended, like I'm some sort of annoying bug, and instead of answering me, he says, "The menu here is really rather limited, isn't it?" And then before I can stab him through the heart with my fork, the waiter shows up with the mineral water and he gets all charming again!

(She sighs. Her cleaning has mostly amounted to shoving piles of things into closets, or under the bed. She now pulls out an over-sized t-shirt and proceeds to get undressed, ready for bed.)

I mean it's not my fault he said he'd go on a date with a woman. Then I thought, well, maybe he's mad at me 'cause he's mad at his mom, who he can't tell the simple facts of his life to.

(The phone rings. She answers it.)

Hello? Hellooo? B.J., for heaven's sake, buy a decent cellphone.

(She hangs up and tosses the phone on the bed.)

So anyway, me and this guy were getting pretty pissy with each other. I had no moments when I thought of him as a fellow traveler, that's for damn sure. At one point I finally decided that he mostly came on this bad date so that he could get a free meal at restaurant he'd heard of, and I decided that I was going to make him pay for the whole thing, full price, and then act surprised that he didn't know that was the deal ahead of time. So there we are on dessert—yes of course even as hideous as the whole date has turned out to be, he of course has to order dessert and keep it all going for an extra half hour—so he's digging into his creme brulee. So I'm sitting there, thinking about how to signal Eileen, to get her to bring over a check. Now I know that Eileen assumes there is no check. Why would she make up a check for me? I would only rip it up. But I am really thinking by this point, this asshole is not going to be rude to me all night, and then get off with a free meal. No fucking way. But I also don't want it to be obvious that I am pulling a devious maneuver, I don't want to stand up, go to Eileen, whisper to her angrily, point at the jerk, and then send her over with a whopping bill for this terrible date. I want to be more subtle than that so that the burden of this delightful embarrassment falls completely, and unexpectedly, on my wretched companion. So I casually lean over, as if I'm just casually looking around the restaurant, and I casually try to spot Eileen to give her some sort of bizarre message with my eyebrows: This guy's an asshole, nothing is on the house, bring the check.

(She makes the bizarre face, to show.)

And Eileen looks at me and goes like this.

(She makes one of those what are you doing faces and gestures.)

And I'm like—

(She makes another ridiculous face, showing how she tried to communicate with Eileen, all the way across the room.)

She doesn't get it. In the heat of the moment, I cannot imagine what her problem is, so I make a bigger face.

(She does.)

So there I am, I've turned my head so that everybody in the room can

see me, except for Mr. Columbia law professor, and I'm making this
incredibly childish, hideous face that's meant to communicate all sorts
of ridiculous nonsense, I mean, I'm virtually —

*(She makes a huge face now, hideous, and points, as if to someone
across the table from her.)*

And who walks in right in, right in the front door, while I'm perform-
ing, for everyone, who should walk in my restaurant at that very moment   but—Mr.   Let's-hope-all-sentient-beings-someday-come-to-
enlightenment. The Bug Guy. *(Beat.)* I am not kidding. This is what I
look like.

(She makes another face, looking quite like a bug.)

He sees this. He waves. Stunned, I wave back. He takes this as an in-
vitation, and comes over to our table.

(She puts her head down for a moment, moaning.)

"Hellooooo," says wretched companion, practically squealing, because, as I think I mentioned before, Bug Guy is very cute, when he's
not talking about bugs. And Bug Guy is also not shy. He pulls up a
chair. He's in the neighborhood, saw my restaurant, remembered my
spectacularly soggy performance at the Buddhist book benefit, apparently, and decided to stop in and see how my spiritual evolution was
coming along! Ugh. So, I introduce them, and bug guy gets all excited
because he's actually heard of Mr. Columbia law professor, who is
both mean and famous, apparently! So in no time at all, Bug Guy and
Wretched Companion are talking about politics and music and litera-
ture and all the things I dreamed of talking about on my dream date
with a man who turned out to be gay.

(The phone rings. She picks it up.)

B.J.? Is that you? Who is this? Bibi? Bibi, cut it out!

(She hangs up quickly, takes a breath and gets it together.)

Uh oh. I may have done something rather ... stupid. Whatever. Anyway. That is why, frankly, I felt the need to apologize to the men tonight. Because wretched companion was one of those guys who act like all women are stupid or something, and it made me feel so bad, and I would hate it if I started to act like that. So I did not stick him with that check. I didn't! You know what? Excuse me.

(She goes to her desk, and opens a drawer. After a moment of quickly looking through a pile of business cards, she selects one, consults it and dials the phone again. She is clearly nervous.)

(Continuing; on phone.) Hi. It's Haley. Haley Walker? Yes. Um ... I would like to see you. Could I see you?

(Blackout.)

SCENE 4

(HALEY's bedroom is much cleaner. She is wearing a robe over devastating lingerie, and she is practically purring.)

I went on a good date. No. I didn't go on a good date. I went on several good dates. More than two. I know, I know you may think that's impossible, that I would ever find a man who I could deem worthy, but I have done it. I have found a good man. *(Beat.)* Monty.

(She laughs.)

Remember Monty? The bad guy from Mildred Pierce! His name's not
Monty, his name is Lewis. I like that name, don't you? Lewis. Elegant
but accessible at the same time, Lewis. Like an Armani suit, in which,
I might add, he looks fantastic. Because this is what happened: After
my hideous date with the nasty gay law professor deteriorated into
okay, abysmal behavior, on my part, I felt that it was time to take
drastic action. I mean, who is in charge here? I am! So I am going to
call somebody who I am interested in having a date with, and I am
going to ask him out. I am going to call Monty. I haven't seen him in
five years, and I presume he's married by now, or at least moved on,
but I am going to take a shot. Why not just take a shot?

So I call him. And I say, I would like to see you, and I invite him to
stop by the restaurant for a drink. He agrees. So on the appointed day
I'm in there, before the dinner rush, and I ask Eileen to make me a
fresh lime vodka gimlet, which she does extremely well, I think she
puts triple sec in it, I can't remember, but it's delicious. Anyway, I am
relaxing in the bar with my delicious cocktail, when this incredible
man walks in the door.

(She laughs, delighted.)

I didn't recognize him at first, I was just thinking who is this, and then
he sees me and he smiles.

(She stands up and does a little dance.)

He smiles at me! He's thrilled to see me! He comes over and tells me
how great I look, what have I been doing, I'm sitting there trying to
think straight, wondering what the hell I was thinking when I walked
away from this? I had some massively ill-conceived theory about Mildred Pierce running through my head, is all I can recall. Well I can't
go into that, of course, so I just say, what have you been doing, and so
he talks, for a little while, about his work, and then he says How's

your daughter? So I tell him about Vera and how big she's getting and he says, She probably doesn't need quite as much of your attention, anymore, and then I think oh lord, he understood what happened. And then he says Are you seeing anybody? And I say, no, how about you?

And he says he was but it kind of went south, and I'm thinking, then she was a big fat moron, oh well so was I—and then he says well, I'm really glad you called. And then he goes.

(A beat.)

He just—leaves the bar. He just came in, talked to me for ten minutes and left. I mean, I knew I had just said a drink, but the drink was going well! I had found, again, this wonderful man, who I once carelessly tossed aside with the same kind of stupid thinking I have relentlessly mocked in others. Remember, the guy who kept wanting to see the end of the movie and how dumb I thought he was? I was just as dumb, what was I thinking, Mildred Pierce? What does Mildred Pierce have to do with anything? They should never let any of us go to the movies. They really shouldn't.

(She paces, restless.)

So my head is in a state. And then of course there's this other stuff that I can't go into, let me just say that work, as much fun as it is to run a restaurant, the restaurant world is not necessarily always the simplest snake pit to negotiate, and it has frankly occurred to me more than once that if a good man showed up to take me way from all this it wouldn't entirely—that's not to say that I'm secretly a fifties girl, just that some days—whatever.

(She shakes her head, paces.)

So the next day he called. He called! And he said, would you like to have dinner. And I said yes. He picked the restaurant, not mine, there was no discussion, he just picked a very good restaurant, Italian, in Brooklyn of all places but it was surprisingly—of course I've heard that about Brooklyn, it's nowhere near as bad as you think.

So he picks me up in his car. Okay, who gets picked up for a date in New York in a car? No one. It was like being in high school again, and I was so nervous, to be in a car, with a man who I had such powerful feelings about, I mean, I am really attracted to this guy, and he is so in charge. I was positively silenced by all of it. I just felt, for fifteen minutes, I felt potentially safe, and I didn't want to say the wrong thing and ruin it.

(She thinks about this.)

So we get to the restaurant, which is perfect, small, maybe thirty set-ups, spectacular Venetian glass chandelier which you might have thought would be too big for such a small space, but just wasn't, pressed tin ceiling that's distressed, I usually don't like that kind of rustic ruin look, but the chandelier contradicted it beautifully. And the food was out of this world, in Brooklyn! So I asked, well of course I asked, the chef trained at Union Square and Lutece, then spent three years in Venice, where she met her husband, the Italian maitre'd with dimples and an accent. Anyway, the rabbit with olives and soft polenta is beyond brilliant; Lewis had the beef cheeks which were also superb. So the food is great, the room is charming, and Lewis is—it's not just him; it's both of us, together, it's magical, I know that sounds trite, but it wasn't trite. It was as if time just evaporated, and everything that had been there for us five years ago was there again, only it was even more wonderful because we had let it slip away, so it was like all those lost hours and days and months were just hovering somewhere in the background, like an echo, of of of loneliness, we were in the middle of something that was just the opposite of being lonely, and it was such a relief, that we both couldn't stop laughing.

We talked until midnight, shut the place down. I can't even remember what we talked about, it was just a blur of happiness. And then we left and drove all over the city and then we parked.

We parked up by the George Washington Bridge and made out in the car for two hours, I kid you not. The next day Vera said to me what happened to your face? It was completely all chapped up, I would have been mortified but I was just too damn happy.

(She paces some more, restless and happy.)

So then I spent the whole morning thinking about having sex, and then I spent lunchtime thinking, Haley, you got to put the brakes on, then Lewis called, and the brakes went off, and then we hung up, and the brakes went back on, and then B.J. called and he thinks everybody should have sex constantly, so the brakes went back off in a big way, and then Lewis called again, and we talked for an hour and the brakes were way off and then I hung up and the brakes went back on. And I was definitely back in high school. You know, the good part of high school, just feeling on fire with things and hopeful and moody, and wanting to buy shoes all the time.

(She pulls a beautiful new pair of shoes out of a box, waves them around gleefully, then puts them on.)

Anyway, then we went out again, to this fantastic place—the most romantic little sushi joint you ever saw, and I am not someone who generally considers sushi romantic. And then we went out a third time. And we didn't go to a restaurant, we just met in the park in the middle of the day and had the most delicious hot dogs I have ever had in my life, and we talked some more and both of us admitted that it was frightening, a bit, how far things had gone, even though we hadn't even slept together yet. And I said, why don't you come over? Let's just stop thinking about it and get it over with! And he said he

had appointments, he had to go back to work, but that we would tomorrow night. And now, tomorrow is here. It's here. Tomorrow is
tonight.

*(She looks at herself in the mirror for a long moment. Then, suddenly,
she moves to the bed, reaches for the phone and dials.)*

Hey, it's me. No, not yet, he's coming over tonight. B.J.—stop it, I'm
too nervous, you can't make fun of me right now. Yes. Ha ha. Yes, of
course I got rid of her, she's spending the night at Emily's. No, honey,
he more than assumes, it's been stated specifically, the plan is that he
comes over, we order Chinese take out and then actually do the deed
on the living room floor before the food even gets here. *(She laughs.)*
What? I guess. *(She checks her watch, moves, nervous.)* A little.
(Beat.) A little, just a little, don't make a big thing, it's a little. Okay,
an hour, he's almost an hour late, but—oh don't do that silence thing.
He's a busy guy, sometimes he's late. I'm not going to turn into one
of those psycho girlfriends who thinks the worst when a guy's a little
late. *(Beat.)* Shit. *(Beat.)* You think I should call him? It's just an
hour. Of course I should call him. It's probably fine, right—yes I have
his home number, I have his cell. I am not being stupid—B.J., stop it,
would you—well, I will, I will call him. I will. Yes, I'll call you back
of course I'll call you back.

(She hangs up the phone.)

(Continuing; to herself.) Jerk.

(She paces now, nervous, picks up the phone, and starts to dial.)

(Continuing; on phone.) Yeah, hi, Lewis? Uh, it's Haley, I was just
wondering what happened to you. So, just I'll give me a call when
you get this, or you maybe I'll see you first. You're probably on your
way. Okay. Bye.

(She hangs up, embarrassed at herself, puts the phone down. After a moment, she sits on the floor, putting her head between her legs, hyperventilating a little.)

Shit. Shit.

(She stands and moves around the room, nervous.)

He's just late. People are late all the time. I am late all the time, all the time, that's so not true, I am never late, I'm too paranoid to be late.

(She goes out into the hallway. After a moment, she returns with a phonebook, sets it on the bed and opens it.)

Be here be here be here—yes.

(She finds the number, shuts the book, and dials. Pause.)

Oh. Hello! Ah, hello, I was wondering, is, um, Lewis there? *(Beat.)* Uh, Haley.

(There is a long beat. She looks up at the ceiling, trying to hold back tears, suddenly.)

Yes, hello, Lewis. I uh, was wondering what happened to you, I think we said eight o'clock, and—Uh huh. Oh. Uh huh. *(Beat.)* Yeah, no of course, I'm not—angry, I'm disappointed, that's all. But not, I just, uh…. Listen, can I just ask, does that have anything to do with the woman who answered the phone? *(Beat.)* You did, yes, you told me about her but you said that you had, that that had "gone south", and—

(There is a pause. HALEY listens and nods her head.)

Oh. Oh! You're living together. No, I, I'm sorry, I didn't understand

that. I thought, "Went South" meant, "Went South." *(Quick beat.)*
I'm not—accusing, oh Jesus, that's so— Listen, it's fine, I don't, I
just thought something else was going on which obviously was my
mistake. But I do, you know, I don't quite understand, why you didn't
call. I mean, it sounds like you came to this decision sometime before
this very instant. So my point being, were you even going to call and
tell me about it? I mean, I've been waiting here for an hour and a half,
expecting you to come over for some big romantic—and you clearly
had no plans to come and were you just going to let me figure that out
on my own in the most humiliating way possible? Okay, yeah, I guess
I am angry, I—

*(She stops herself, trying not to lose it. After a moment, she takes a
    breath.)*

You know what? I don't want to talk about this anymore. I have to
go. And don't come into my restaurant, even if someone as stupid
as me calls you and invites you, don't even think about it, because
you know what? We don't serve lying deceitful cheating fucking
cowards.

*(She hangs up the phone. She goes into the bathroom, where she sobs
    good and hard, then comes back out, with a Kleenex.)*

Well. That makes me the biggest idiot on the planet. I'm not an idiot.
He lied, he was just a fucking liar, and I'm a fucking idiot because I
didn't see it. Well, people lie to you in new and exciting ways all the
time, I guess.

(She sees her shoes then takes them off, puts them back in their box.)

Oh, god. Now I'm never going to be able to wear these shoes without
feeling like shit and they cost me four hundred dollars. Well, that's
too bad. They're pretty, too. *(Beat.)* How the hell did I not see that?

Guy takes me all the way to Brooklyn for dinner because he's a big old romantic? Like, it didn't even occur to me that maybe he didn't want to be caught? My powers of delusion are really noteworthy. Brooklyn.

(The phone rings. She turns to look at it, exhausted, and then goes to pick it up.)

Listen B.J., I can't talk right now. *(Beat.)* Who is this? Eileen? Eileen, you are not going to believe what just happened to me, I just feel like shit, so—what? I can't hear you, what— *(Beat.)* Shit.

(She sits down.)

What did he say? *(Beat.)* No no don't give him the phone, don't— *(Sudden shift in voice.)* Hi, hi Veljko, how you doing? Wow, it's amazing to hear from you. Yeah, yes, we've been working hard, it's, the place is really humming and—so when'd you get out?

(She listens, nodding.)

Mmmm hmmm. Mmmmmm. Yes well listen, I fired Bibi because he was stealing, Veljko, it had gotten real—no, no—did he tell you that?

Because that is completely, uh—Veljko, Veljko, look, there's no point in getting worked up over what some third party has told you, I'd be happy to walk you through the books, that's not a problem. Why don't you come by tomorrow afternoon, I was gonna be in about— *(Beat.)* No, actually I'm not doing anything right now. You want me to come in right now, sure I can do that. *(Beat.)* No, you don't need to send anybody. I'll be there in half an hour. Yeah, I understand that, Veljko. I'll be there.

(She hangs up the phone and sits, silent.)

Well, this is turning out to be quite a night. *(She starts to move, fast now.)* As I said before, I have in fact done some rather stupid things in the name of survival which may in fact have been even more unwise than I first suspected.

(She changes clothes, quickly, into jeans a sweatshirt.)

The fact is, and this is a fact worth knowing, the only reason for a restaurant to have a cash-only policy is for purposes of tax evasion and, um, in addition, possibly, money laundering, as I reported earlier. Not that I have been, on the contrary, but in addition to the aforementioned activities, it is possible to, how shall I put this. Cash only business, it's pretty easy to start dipping into the till.

(She goes to the bed, takes out the shoebox full of money, sets it on the bed, opens it, dumps it into a bag.)

It's just, a temptation for someone who's on her own and trying to be capable, it's not always easy for a single woman to be just capable without resorting to criminal behavior.

I mean, I am not the first woman who stretched the legality of any given situation. Mildred Pierce, right?

(She takes two big books out from under the bed, goes to the closet, pulls out some really practical shoes and puts them on quickly. She picks up the phone and dials.)

(Continuing; bright.) Emily? Hi, it's Vera's mom, can I talk to her? Thanks. *(Beat.)* Hi, honey. No, everything's great. Oh. Yeah, he's here, we're having Chinese food, everything's great. But now listen, sweetie, I have to come pick you up, okay? No, nothing serious, it's just some things have come up so I have to come get you and you should be dressed, all right. Vera, really, I can't—I CANNOT AR-

GUE ABOUT THIS, VERA. I'M COMING TO GET YOU NOW.

(She stops herself, sudden. Bites her lip.)

 I'm sorry. I'm sorry, sweetie. I'll tell you about it when I get there. Everything's fine, but I have to come get you, and um, wait upstairs, okay? Don't, just tell Emily's mom I'll come up. Don't wait downstairs. I'll come up. *(Beat.)* I love you, too.

(She hangs up the phone.)

It's fine. I'm not afraid. Everything's fine.

(She picks up the wads of cash from the bed, shoves them into her purse, grabs her coat and goes. Blackout.)

SCENE 5

(The following morning. HALEY stands at the window, letting the light stream over her. She wears the same clothing from the night before, and looks exhausted.)

I was used to doing things by myself. What is that thing they always talk about, one of the things people sometimes like about Americans, is their rugged independence. Pull yourself up by your bootstraps. Don't be a big baby, ever. There's nothing wrong with that except that when you make a mistake you're on your own. Because that's the way you made your life.

(She sits, starts to take off her shoes, exhausted.)

The thing is, they eventually went back to it. The money laundering?

Those Romanians? Not that they involved me. I ran the restaurant, they let me do what I needed to do to make that place hum, that was just a front to them, they didn't care. But I did. And they weren't paying their taxes. They weren't protecting the restaurant. So if the feds ever came back, they could shut the whole place down. Seventeen people work in that place. That's not counting me. We all built it together. So—I kept another set of books, myself. And I paid the taxes behind their backs. So that if the law ever did show up again, and those nice criminals, who let me run my own restaurant, if they ever got in trouble again, the restaurant would be safe. That's how it started. I was paying the taxes. And then—okay. It went a little further than that. I have a kid. I wanted her in a good school, and you know, you have this kid, you want to give her things. A nice coat, once in a while. A drum set at Christmas. Although, the drum set was a mistake.

(She starts to take her clothes off.)

But it was mostly for the taxes. Some of the waiters knew. Eileen always knew. One of the cooks. I don't think anyone deliberately ratted me out to that little piece of shit Bibi, nobody liked him. But somehow, unbeknownst to me, he put two and two together. Believe me, if I knew he knew, I would not have fired his sorry ass.

It was risky anyway, because he's related to all those Romanians, but I was pretty sick of him, it was a risk I was willing to take. I just didn't count on Veljko getting out of prison at this opportune moment. I knew he was getting out soon, I was nervous about that, but I didn't know when. And then—it had gone so far for so many years, there was no way you could explain. "I've been stealing from the business to pay the taxes." Try saying that to a criminal. So last night when he called …

(She thinks about this.)

I didn't have a lot of choices. I didn't have anybody to go to. So, I was gonna run. I was gonna grab my kid and catch a train and go. That's what I did before. When Roger turned into such a psychopath. Just get out of town. Go start someplace new. No one's gonna help you. You don't have anyone to help you.

(She stands, tries to shake this off.)

So I don't know why I went to the cops instead. I truly do not know, and I also do not know, and did not know at the time, if what I had done would get me in trouble with them as well as with the Romanian mafia. What a lovely position to be in. Maybe the cops will try to arrest me, I have after all been stealing. Maybe the feds will arrest me. Or maybe they'll just take all the information I have on criminal activity down at Romanian mob central, and then send me and my child back to my apartment, where the minions of the Romanian mafia would be waiting for us. I didn't know. So I don't know why I went there. Maybe I just needed to believe, finally, that there was help, you don't have to be alone, we live together in this huge city, so many of us, there has to be help out there. And why shouldn't it be the police? That's their job! So I show up, hysterical, looking like a sexually frustrated wreck, dragging an angry and frightened twelve year girl, and babbling on about the Romanian mafia—it wasn't my most impressive moment.

I think they would have most definitely tossed me back onto the street, had I not dumped fifteen thousand dollars in small bills all over somebody's dirty desk. Really, those police precincts are filthy, that's not something they just make up on television.

(She goes to the door.)

Vera, did you offer him coffee? Offer him coffee, and don't put those extra scoops in, that's just for me. Other people don't drink it like that.

(She goes to the bathroom, comes out with a toothbrush and tooth-paste.)

So once I had their attention, things really started to rock. They take Vera somewhere, sit her in a corner and feed her ice cream and coke all night, that's what she told me later, you got to wonder about the common sense of something like that, but I didn't know anything about it at the time. 'Cause I'm off in one of those interrogation rooms and people are asking me this and that, names of people, how much money over the years, how much I knew, somebody brings in one of those mug books—those also look exactly like they do on television. I have to say, my whole experience sort of reassured me about what we're seeing on television, those cop shows are actually pretty accurate. Anyway, at some point one of them, this kind of round cop, says, you know, you maybe want to think about getting yourself a lawyer. And he says it kind of casual, and I was suddenly so afraid. 'Cause I remembered something else I learned from all those cop shows: Get the lawyer. I just remembered everybody always wanting the perps or the witnesses or whoever to never get a lawyer and the one stupid thing was not getting a lawyer. So I said, yes, I want that. Then there was more whispering and talking and then the round one says, due respect? You don't want a public defender. You're gonna need somebody good. And I just felt sick. I don't know any lawyers. It must have been three in the morning by then. I was so tired. They let me see Vera, at which point I became aware that they had been pumping her full of sugar for hours, so I told them to cut that out.

And she said to me, what's going on, Mom, and I just held her hand and said, everything's fine. The biggest problem we got right now is you explaining to me how you can eat like that and not vomit on your shoes! And so she's kind of laughing with me about that, and holding onto me at the same time, and I'm just sitting there, resting, trying hard not to lose it, when who should walk in the front door of that dirty police station, but—the Bug Guy.

(Beat. She wipes her eyes.)

I kid you not. They decided I needed somebody good, that's the kind of mess I was in, and so that nice cop called one of his friends, who happened to be—the Bug Guy. Who's a lawyer. Which is how come he knew Mr. Columbia Law Professor, remember that? So there he is, in my hour of need. The Bug Guy. And I sat there, and I thought—there's something bigger going on here. I'm sorry. Please don't think I've lost my mind. It's been a long night. The Bug Guy—his name is—aw, I'm not going to tell you what his name is—he sits down next to me and says, hi, how you doing? Like it's the most normal thing in the world to see someone you met in a Buddhist thunderstorm, at three in the morning in a police station. And I say, I'm fine, how are you? And he says, is this Vera? And I say, it is. And he introduces himself as a friend of mine, just came down when he heard I might need someone to talk to and that he was going to take us home. Like it was so clear and simple and not a problem, none of this, whatever mess I was in was just not a problem. He was so peaceful—well, he's kind of a peaceful guy, did I mention that? Maybe you assumed that, because of the Buddhist thing, or maybe you just thought he was a nut, that's what I thought—anyway, he just cuts through there and takes me right into the office of the chief, and he says, she's cooperating but she needs protection. Veljko gets picked up right now on the evidence she's already given, she doesn't take the stand, and however you work this, nothing comes back to her.

Then the chief starts to argue, but the Bug Guy, he's so calm, he just explains it all and it makes so much sense, we're all just sitting there, calm, and more and more it seems like everybody's going to get what they want, just by being calm. Have you ever heard of a Zen lawyer? It's sort of like Phil Jackson without the sweat. Nobody's sweating. We're all calm. And then even a little cheerful. That's the thing, I always used to think that about those Buddhists whenever I'd see them on the cover of a book or something: They always seem so cheerful. We sure felt cheerful. And they just let me go home. *(Sitting, exhausted.)* I need to go talk to the Bug Guy. My own private Buddhist lawyer. I'm just a ding-a-ling. Remember that first time I met him? When I thought, you know, if you think the Bug Guy is cute, maybe it means it's been too long since you've been on a date? Well maybe that's not what it means. We don't always know what things mean. Your life unfolds. You think you're in the middle of the worst catastrophe imaginable, and then the Bug Guy shows up. It's mysterious. So maybe if you think the Bug Guy is cute, maybe it's because he is cute. Maybe thunderstorms are a gift of the Buddha. Maybe men and women weren't put on earth to torture each other. Maybe we're here because we need each other.

(She thinks about this, yawns.)

I'm going to go have coffee with the Bug Guy.

(She goes. Blackout.)

End of play

Also By

Theresa Rebeck

ABSTRACT EXPRESSION
THE BELLS
THE BUTTERFLY COLLECTION
DOES THIS WOMAN HAVE A NAME
THE FAMILY OF MANN
LOOSE KNIT
MAURITIUS
OMNIUM GATHERUM (with Alexandra Gersten-Vassilaros)
OUR HOUSE
THE SCENE
SPIKE HEELS
SUNDAY ON THE ROCKS
VIEW OF THE DOME
THE WATER'S EDGE

SKIN DEEP
Jon Lonoff

Comedy / 2m, 2f / Interior Unit Set

In *Skin Deep*, a large, lovable, lonely-heart, named Maureen Mulligan, gives romance one last shot on a blind-date with sweet awkward Joseph Spinelli; she's learned to pepper her speech with jokes to hide insecurities about her weight and appearance, while he's almost dangerously forthright, saying everything that comes to his mind. They both know they're perfect for each other, and in time they come to admit it.

They were set up on the date by Maureen's sister Sheila and her husband Squire, who are having problems of their own: Sheila undergoes a non-stop series of cosmetic surgeries to hang onto the attractive and much-desired Squire, who may or may not have long ago held designs on Maureen, who introduced him to Sheila. With Maureen particularly vulnerable to both hurting and being hurt, the time is ripe for all these unspoken issues to bubble to the surface.

"Warm-hearted comedy … the laughter was literally show-stopping.
A winning play, with enough good-humored laughs and sentiment to keep you smiling from beginning to end."
– *TalkinBroadway.com*

"It's a little Paddy Chayefsky, a lot Neil Simon and a quick-witted, intelligent voyage into the not-so-tranquil seas of middle-aged love and dating. The dialogue is crackling and hilarious; the plot simple but well-turned; the characters endearing and quirky; and lurking beneath the merriment is so much heartache that you'll stand up and cheer when the unlikely couple makes it to the inevitable final clinch."
– *NYTheatreWorld.Com*

COCKEYED
William Missouri Downs

Comedy / 3m, 1f / Unit Set
Phil, an average nice guy, is madly in love with the beautiful Sophia. The only problem is that she's unaware of his existence. He tries to introduce himself but she looks right through him. When Phil discovers Sophia has a glass eye, he thinks that might be the problem, but soon realizes that she really can't see him. Perhaps he is caught in a philosophical hyperspace or dualistic reality or perhaps beautiful women are just unaware of nice guys. Armed only with a B.A. in philosophy, Phil sets out to prove his existence and win Sophia's heart. This fast moving farce is the winner of the HotCity Theatre's GreenHouse New Play Festival. The St. Louis Post-Dispatch called Cockeyed a clever romantic comedy, Talkin' Broadway called it "hilarious," while Playback Magazine said that it was "fresh and invigorating."

Winner!
of the HotCity Theatre GreenHouse New Play Festival

"Rocking with laughter...hilarious...polished and engaging work draws heavily on the age-old conventions of farce: improbable situations, exaggerated characters, amazing coincidences, absurd misunderstandings, people hiding in closets and barely missing each other as they run in and out of doors...full of comic momentum as Cockeyed hurtles toward its conclusion."
–Talkin' Broadway

THE OFFICE PLAYS
Two full length plays by Adam Bock

THE RECEPTIONIST
Comedy / 2m, 2f / Interior

At the start of a typical day in the Northeast Office, Beverly deals effortlessly with ringing phones and her colleague's romantic troubles. But the appearance of a charming rep from the Central Office disrupts the friendly routine. And as the true nature of the company's business becomes apparent, The Receptionist raises disquieting, provocative questions about the consequences of complicity with evil.

"...Mr. Bock's poisoned Post-it note of a play."
– *New York Times*

"Bock's intense initial focus on the routine goes to the heart of
The Receptionist's pointed, painfully timely allegory... elliptical,
provocative play..."
– *Time Out New York*

THE THUGS
Comedy / 2m, 6f / Interior

The Obie Award winning dark comedy about work, thunder and the mysterious things that are happening on the 9th floor of a big law firm. When a group of temps try to discover the secrets that lurk in the hidden crevices of their workplace, they realize they would rather believe in gossip and rumors than face dangerous realities.

"Bock starts you off giggling, but leaves you with a chill."
– *Time Out New York*

"... a delightfully paranoid little nightmare that is both more
chillingly realistic and pointedly absurd than anything
John Grisham ever dreamed up."
– *New York Times*

SAMUELFRENCH.COM

NO SEX PLEASE, WE'RE BRITISH
Anthony Marriott and Alistair Foot

Farce / 7 m, 3 f / Interior
A young bride who lives above a bank with her husband who is the assistant manager, innocently sends a mail order off for some Scandinavian glassware. What comes is Scandinavian pornography. The plot revolves around what is to be done with the veritable floods of pornography, photographs, books, films and eventually girls that threaten to engulf this happy couple. The matter is considerably complicated by the man's mother, his boss, a visiting bank inspector, a police superintendent and a muddled friend who does everything wrong in his reluctant efforts to set everything right, all of which works up to a hilarious ending of closed or slamming doors. This farce ran in London over eight years and also delighted Broadway audiences.

"Titillating and topical."
– *NBC TV*

"A really funny Broadway show."
– *ABC TV*

WHITE BUFFALO
Don Zolidis

Drama / 3m, 2f (plus chorus)/ Unit Set

Based on actual events, WHITE BUFFALO tells the story of the miracle birth of a white buffalo calf on a small farm in southern Wisconsin. When Carol Gelling discovers that one of the buffalo on her farm is born white in color, she thinks nothing more of it than a curiosity. Soon, however, she learns that this is the fulfillment of an ancient prophecy believed by the Sioux to bring peace on earth and unity to all mankind. Her little farm is quickly overwhelmed with religious pilgrims, bringing her into contact with a culture and faith that is wholly unfamiliar to her. When a mysterious businessman offers to buy the calf for two million dollars, Carol is thrown into doubt about whether to profit from the religious beliefs of others or to keep true to a spirituality she knows nothing about.

BLUE YONDER
Kate Aspengren

Dramatic Comedy / Monolgues and scenes
12f (can be performed with as few as 4 with doubling) / Unit Set

A familiar adage states, "Men may work from sun to sun, but women's work is never done." In Blue Yonder, the audience meets twelve mesmerizing and eccentric women including a flight instructor, a firefighter, a stuntwoman, a woman who donates body parts, an employment counselor, a professional softball player, a surgical nurse professional baseball player, and a daredevil who plays with dynamite among others. Through the monologues, each woman examines her life's work and explores the career that she has found. Or that has found her.

CPSIA information can be obtained at www.ICGtesting.com
Printed in the USA
LVOW070641250313

325325LV00006B/83/P